My
Heart
Your Soul
MEMORY OF DREAMS

JASON
JAVI
ROSE
CHARACTERS

BEVERLY
CURTIS
LESLIE

"We were gonna tell everyone eventually, but..."
"If it's to hear you try to sing that one song again and mess up horribly, sure."

"Anyway, let's drink to that shall we?!"
"Besides, I can't overshadow a best selling novelist sitting with us."
It truly feels like I never left.

"Javi! Your turn to sing, but first, another round of shots!"
"If you go up to sing, I'll do a duet with you."

I saw a figure in a white dress with angel wings, humming a beautiful melody.

Memories, like dreams, dance on the edges of
consciousness, ethereal and elusive, fading whispe
of emotions that time tries to erase.

De'Shaun J. Ruiz

CONTENTS

DESHAUN J. RUIZ
Cover Art by De'Shaun J. Ruiz

Library of Congress Cataloging-in-Publication Data Available
ISBN: 979-8-9869784-4-4
ISBN: 979-8-9869784-5-1 (ebook)

Find My Heart Your Soul: The Video Game available on steam.com

The Story Thus Far

Two years have passed since Javi laid her mother to rest. When she was twenty-three, she bid farewell to her hometown and all that it encompassed to pursue a new life in the city.

Determined to sever ties with her past, Javi buried herself in her work, hoping to forget the haunting memories that plagued her, but she was mistaken.

While endeavoring to forge ahead, the echoes of her past caught up, and the memories flooded back.

Just as she tried to make sense of everything, an old friend reached out to her, proposing a reunion among high school friends.

With some uncertainty, Javi decided to go, hoping to finally confront what she's been running from all these years.

1

Life can be cruel.

It snatches away what we hold most dear, leaving us to pick up the shattered pieces. Over the years, I slowly came to terms with that reality. But in the midst of my despair, I found sanctuary in the dreams that held my memories and the emotions that kept them alive.

In my dreams, lie my childhood and the time I spent with my parents and friends before everything changed. They feel so vivid that I can sometimes smell the scent of my father's cooking and feel the warmth of my mother's embrace. But dreams can't last forever, and reality always manages to sneak back in.

I woke up from the frigid December air chilling through my apartment. I couldn't help but feel like my sanctuary had been invaded. Its frosty breeze nibbled my toes.

I sat up, noticing the window was slightly ajar. *How could I forget to close it before napping?* I thought to myself.

I rose off the couch, traversing through the towering boxes that were scattered around my living room floor to close the window.

As I glanced outside, the sky was progressively darkening with each passing minute. The winter season always brought a sense of coziness and warmth to me despite the cold weather. Somehow seeing the city covered in snow always took my breath in awe.

The evening sun melted as day and night intersected above the city. The purple hues grew while the warm autumn orange slowly faded away. Bright city lights aglow. Stars began to twinkle. *You can never deny that view.*

For what the condo is worth, this is the reason why I bought it and it's been one of the best decisions I've ever made.

I bought it a few years ago when I was finally able to afford a place of my own. It's not too big, but it's just the right size for me.

The location is perfect too - I'm right in the heart of the city surrounded by skyscrapers and bustling streets. From my window, I can see the cityscape stretching out before me, with all its lights and energy.

I always loved the idea of having a place to call my own, and being able to decorate it the way I want. Of course, buying a condo isn't easy, especially in a city like this.

As a best-selling author, having a space that inspires me is essential. It took me a while to save up enough money from book sales and licensing deals for the full purchase, and even longer to find the right place.

There's something about the hustle and bustle of the city that fuels my creativity. And when I need a break, I can step outside onto my balcony and take in the city's sights and sounds. But more than anything, it's mine.

After all these years moving place to place, I needed a space that felt like home, a place where I could heal and start anew. It's cozy and comfortable, with just enough room for all my books and my writing desk. And since it's mine, I can decorate it however I want.

I've filled it with all my favorite things, from the bright orange couch to the vintage record player from my college days in the dorm room. This place had become my sanctuary, and I feel grateful every day that I get to call it home.

I stepped away from the window to see the progress I made before taking a nap. *Wow, I left such a mess.*

I sat back on the couch, staring at the piles of boxes scattered throughout the space. It's strange how the past can seep into every part of our lives, even when we try our best to leave it behind.

Just earlier today, I was helping my Auntie clear out her garage. She called me the night before about their mice problem and wanted to see if there's anything I wanted before they started throwing stuff away. My Auntie loved throwing out old things. What others see as trinkets, memories, and collectibles, she only saw trash. And now I'm stuck with whatever was left.

Most of it were stuffed with old photo albums and holiday cards from over the years. I donated several boxes of old clothes that were stored from when I was a kid, but there was one box I couldn't bring myself to letting go. And it sat on the glass table in front of me.

I squeezed my eyes shut, turning away, and got to my feet. Even after taking a nap, I still couldn't reopen it.

As much as I wanted to move on and start fresh, the past somehow was always one step ahead of me.

It belonged to my mother.

I was twelve when my father passed. By then, my mother and I slowly started to grow apart. It was like we were on different wavelengths, no longer able to connect with each other.

My mother mostly concentrated all of her energy on her work, leaving me to fend for myself.

If I wasn't with friends, I typically remained in my father's vacant office, engrossed in reading and browsing through old photographs. Being in that room made me feel closer to him, like he was still with me in some way.

She tried to have me understand that he was gone, but I didn't want to hear it. How could I just accept he was taken from me so soon when we had promises left abandoned?

There were brief moments when I did feel reconnected with her, like when we'd share a meal or watch a movie together, but moments like those were fleeting. Life wasn't the same.

It was like we were both struggling to find our way back to each other, but the distance between us became too great.

I remember feeling so lost and alone during those times. I missed my father terribly and wished he was still around to help bridge the gap between my mother and me.

So, after I graduated college, I left. Never saw her since and I never thought to look back - until now.

It's been two years since her passing, and yet she still managed to find a way to reach me after all this time.

I did go to her funeral, wanting to get one last look at her, before she'd forever be placed beside my father in the ground. Part of me thought I'd find closure, but what awaited me was only pain.

That day as I stood there, watching my mother's coffin being lowered into the ground, my heart felt heavy and my mind was in a fog. I hadn't seen or spoken to her in years, and now this was the last time I would ever see her face.

Memories of our falling out flooded my mind, making it hard to breathe. I remembered the hurtful words I exchanged and the distance that grew between us. I wished I could turn back time and fix things, but it was too late now.

Tears streamed down my face as I watched the dirt being shoveled over her coffin. The finality of it all hit me like a ton of bricks. She was really gone, and I would never have the chance to make amends with her.

It made me feel like a teenager again, being overwhelmed with this adolescent grief. It was a feeling I swore I had left behind after moving, but here it was, raw and unrelenting.

When the last of the dirt was packed down, I whispered a final goodbye. Even though our relationship had been strained, my emotions made aware that she would always hold a special place in my heart. I knew that I would have to find a way to live with the regret of never having the chance to make things right.

When I first opened the box in the garage, her pile of "Return to Sender" letters were the first things I pulled out. I still haven't even read those yet. I've already acknowledged it's too late.

No matter how many unread voicemails and letters appeared to haunt me, I kept telling myself I'd never look back. That was until I saw one white envelope that stuck out to me as I was scrounging through earlier.

There wasn't a mailing address nor a sending address on it. Only two words written in her handwriting: *For Javi.*

Why did she never send this one? I thought. Then, the curiosity drove me to open it right away.

Of all the letters, why did this one feel different from the rest? The back of the envelope was sealed with a red stamp in the shape of a heart.

I gently opened it, without tear, and the contents inside were only a folded sheet of paper and a white gold heart necklace with a heart shaped tourmaline on the left side and an amethyst on the other. Engraved on both sides, at the top of the heart, were two names. On the right was Javi, which is my name of coarse, and on the other was a name of someone I don't know: Leah.

The contents of the letter is what reopened a hole in my heart I thought I had finally closed.

I clenched the necklace in my hands, reading what I felt were my mothers final words to me she never got to speak - her regrets, her wishes, her tears that dried on the edge of the letter.

I never expected to find a letter from her that would change everything I perceived of my past.

Deep down, I still feel the loneliness and regret. My mind couldn't stop wishing things were different between us. I wanted her to understand how I felt, and she wanted me to let go.

Like I said, I've already acknowledged long ago that it's too late, but reading her heart written onto the page made me wish it wasn't.

I stood in front of the mirror beside my bed, my fingers tracing the delicate chain that lay around my neck. The reflection of myself stared back at me, holding my emotions back. I clutched the heart necklace close to my chest and took a deep breath.

As I held it in my hands, I couldn't help but feel a sense of longing and sadness wash over me. I envisioned my mother's face reflected back - her smile, her laughter, her warmth. Beside me, the digital clock on my dresser read the time.

5:15PM.

"Shit!"

Panicking, I rushed to my closet picking through clothes. I had no time to find a nice outfit so I tried to see what matched with the white tee and jeans I already had on.

There were various styles of clothing to choose from that surely enough some I've never worn and should donate. Shirts, pants, dresses, skirts - it was all there, a chaotic mess of colors and fabrics.

I sighed and began to shift through the piles, searching for something to wear for my night out with friends. But the more I looked, the more overwhelming it got.

Everything seemed either too casual or too fancy. I held up a sequined dress, but quickly put it back - it was definitely too elegant plus it's cold.

I groaned in frustration, wondering why I couldn't just have a simple, go-to outfit like some of my friends. I kept tossing hangers holding jackets, coats, and fancy dresses aside onto my bed.

"I'm going to be late!!!"

Sitting on the last hangar was a grey sweater. I'm not sure if I ever worn it yet, but it goes well with my jeans and socks and the best option at the moment.

I quickly put it on, along with my brown boots, and rush to the door. *I can't miss this train!*

I quickly rushed out the door, my heart pounding with fear and anxiety.

As I grabbed my favorite green overcoat, I took a deep breath and ran toward the station, hoping I'd make it on time.

2

Chooooooooo!

The train whistle roared while steadily increasing speed, leaving the station.

I stood on the train platform of my hometown, utterly astonished. *I'm back.* Who would've thought I'd find myself here again.

It's a small suburban town surrounded by wilderness located two hours from the city. If anyone wanted to find a place for peace and quiet, but still have the nightlife excitement, this was it.

I stepped down the stairs, taking in the senses. I couldn't help but feel a wave of nostalgia wash over me. The sound of snow crunching beneath my feet brought back memories I thought I forgot.

Having lived in the city for so long, you tend to forget that refreshing sensation of wilderness air breathed into your lungs and the lack of sirens wailing in the night.

My childhood memories began to flood back like distant dreams of a time so long ago that I found myself questioning in disbelief whether they had truly occurred.

I remember walking hand in hand with my parents through these streets, feeling their warmth and love.

The cozy nights we spent at home where my mother read me stories while my father cooked our favorite meals. We would sit by the television, sipping hot cocoa and sharing our days.

One winter, my mom and I baked cookies. I can still smell the sweet scent of vanilla and sugar filling the air.

But now, as I stand here watching the snow fall, I can't help but feel a deep sense of loss. My parents are no longer here, and I can never go back to those carefree days of my childhood. It's as if a part of me has been frozen in time, forever trapped in the recollections of what once was.

"Where are they?"

It was already fifteen minutes past seven. I frequently checked the time on my phone, trying to keep my hands in my jacket pockets. It's freezing.

Meanwhile, passengers were getting picked up and leaving the station wearing festive winter attire. There was laughter amidst the flurry of activity as travelers exchanged hugs, adding to the warm holiday atmosphere.

Tonight is the town's winter festival and I was supposed to meet up with my childhood friends from school. I haven't seen them in years, but the winter festival was the perfect opportunity to reconnect.

I couldn't help feeling nervous of our reunion. Figures I'd be late and they're probably already drinking and telling old stories without me.

Bzzzt.

I quickly sacrificed a hand to the bitter cold winds to check my phone. It was a text:

Hey! Did you make it to the station?

Before I could read who sent it, I felt a tap on my shoulder. Startled, I looked behind me seeing none other than Jason, greeting me with a gentle wave and a large grin on his face.

"Did you get my text?"

Not one word came out of my mouth as I immediately wrapped my arms around his waist.

For a moment, I didn't recognize him; it had been so long since we had seen each other in person. His hazel brown hair flared back with ear muffs and lean figure dressed with a black overcoat.

If it wasn't for the fact I haven't seen him in so long, I would've smacked him for scaring me.

"I didn't get the chance to respond back," I said, hugging him longer than I should have.

I let go, fixing my composure, and gave him a nice nudge on the shoulder. This being our first interaction in person after all these years, I can't be surprised it would turned out like this.

We first met in middle school. Back then, I was a very shy girl. Most people were able to make friends easily, but not so much for me.

My dad always encouraged me to make friends and to never force what will come naturally.

As the school year continued and people had their friend groups, I was still sitting in the back corner alone at lunch. Then one day, Jason sat across from me.

At first, I pegged him as some tomboy, who gets angry easily, sporting these black studs and masculine personality being pranked by the athletes he'd hang out with into sitting across the loner kid, but I was wrong. He just wanted a true friend.

His lack of restraint and open personality grew on me so much, I got used to having him around at school. Despite mostly showing others a tough exterior at times, Jason has a really soft and caring side. He was always friendly and eager to make friends, which initially intimidated me at first. Ever since then, we became inseparable.

We would often spend our afternoons at my house playing video games, watching movies, and having sleepovers. It was so much fun creating imaginary worlds and acting out our favorite scenes from movies. We would laugh and joke around, and I felt like I could be myself around him.

As we got older, our interests kinda went in different directions, but we still hung out whenever we could. He really had my back during some tough times. We'd talk for hours on the phone, and Jason always knew how to make me feel better.

After I left, we tried to stay connected. We kept planning to meet up, but with me moving away and getting crazy busy, I ended up being the one with hardly any time.

"I'm just glad to see you made it." His warm smile kept breaking down my facade at being mad for scaring me. Jason knew how to get passed my emotional defenses, and honestly, I never minded.

Honk. Honk.

Both of us turned around to see a car sitting in the pick-up lane. The front passenger window rolled down and a woman with long black hair stuck her head out.

"Come on! Let's go!" She waved. "Curtis can't leave the car parked here for too long."

"You don't have to shout that loud Beverly, roll up the window the heat is on!"

Were they here this entire time? It's a white compact crossover SUV so it kind of blends in with the snow and all the other various white cars people drive around anyway.

I looked at Jason whose clearly trying to pretend that I haven't pieced together the fact he stood out in the cold winds of winter, waiting for me, while everyone else stayed warm in Curtis's car.

"I shall plead the fifth." Jason whistled all guilty.

Honk. Honk.

"It's cold!"

3

The town felt alive with the spirit of the winter festival - twinkling lights, festive music and food stands at every corner of the block.

Traffic was being redirected constantly due to the ongoing parade, but it was cool to see all the parade floats go by with the marching bands playing down the street. The parade wasn't this huge when I was little.

We were on our way to the heart of town, where majority of the winter festival was happening. The colorful lights and festive music filled the air, creating a lively and cheerful atmosphere that was infectious.

Leslie and Rose occupied the back seat, their heads bent together in an animated discussion and occasional shared smiles. Jason was sitting next to me, tapping his foot to the beat of the music outside, admiring the elaborate parade floats that passed by.

Up front, Beverly was busy pointing out all the different activities and booths that we should check out later while Curtis was expertly navigating through the crowds, making sure we didn't get stuck in any traffic jams.

"Wow, everything looks so different," I said, peering out the window at the brightly lit buildings and festive decorations.

When I was younger, this place was just growing with several shops but now it's a bazaar full of small businesses, high-end restaurants, and pubs.

Leslie grinned. "At least Gogi Byeokje is still around. You know how many people would be mad if that place closed down?"

Gogi Byeokje was our favorite restaurant to hang out when we would be home for the summer from college.

The smell of high quality marinated meat being grilled at the table where we could essentially cook it ourselves was it's top selling point that got many people in the building.

"Thank goodness for that," I responded.

Beverly leaned back from the passenger seat, a reminiscent smile crossing her lips. "Hey, ya'll remember that spot! Curtis would get those thick corn beef sandwiches. I'll never forget the time he spilled mustard on his favorite sweater trying to take that giant bite."

"I don't know how you'd eat those," Rose remarked.

"They're not bad if you give it a try." Curtis chimed from behind the wheel, his face slightly reddening and embarrassment evident in his voice. He took advantage of the red light to respond, then added, "Oh by the way, there's still some time before our table reservation. Do you guys want to walk around and check out the festivities?"

Rose's eyes lit up with excitement. "Yes! I want to see the ice sculptures and try some of the food from the vendors."

Jason, who had been quietly snoozing away until now, spoke up. "Sounds like a plan to me. Might as well have a blast while we're here."

As we parked the car and stepped out into the chilly air, I couldn't help but feel grateful for my friends who had been by my side since childhood.

The decision to come back, maybe against the odds, suddenly seemed right. There was a comfort in their company that made everything feel invigorating, a feeling that whispered I was exactly where I belonged. *Maybe it was the right call to comeback.*

***

We made our way to the main square, where a giant ice rink had been set up. My friends laced up their skates with practiced ease, while I fumbled awkwardly, trying not to let my nerves get the best of me. But as soon as I stepped onto the ice, I was engulfed with a sense of joy that I hadn't felt in years.

We skated and laughed, twirling and spinning on the ice, until our cheeks were rosy and our fingers numb with cold. We took a break and headed over to the hot cocoa stand, savoring the sweet, rich flavor and warming our hands around the cups.

As we explored the festival, I couldn't help but feel a sense of nostalgia for the times I had spent here with my parents. We'd walk around these very streets, participate in the annual scavenger hunt, and eat all kinds of festive foods. But there was one year that stood out to me in particular.

I must have been around 7 or 8 years old, and I remember this desire to make a wish at the tree during its first light. I got the idea mostly from a story my mom would tell me every Christmas before bed about a person's wish coming true if done at the exact moment the tree first lights the town. It wasn't the first time I had this sort of ambition, but something about that time I wanted my wish to come true.

In that moment, I stood in front of the big Christmas tree looking up at the sparkling ornaments. My eyes closed with determination, I only had one thought in mind and made my wish. I wished for a sister.

I remember feeling so lonely sometimes and I thought having a sister would make everything better. I remembered telling my parents about my wish and how excited I was for it to come true. But it never did.

My mother had postpartum complications after I was born that having another child would've been a huge risk to take hence my wish was left unfulfilled.

I was too young back then to have known the truth as to why. Sometimes I still think about it to this exact moment, wondering what life would have been like if somehow my wish did come true. Would my sister and I be close? What would her personality had been like?

During that period of my life, that was my only desire. However, over time, it evolved into a longing for my parents to never depart from my side.

When my father's illness started showing its first signs, the fear of being alone and losing them made me wish for their constant presence and to never leave me. In hindsight, this wish appeared straightforward, but back then, it held immense significance to me.

Now, as I glanced around, sharing laughter, jokes, and capturing silly photos in the festival photo booth, a profound sense of tranquility washed over me.

It felt as though I was reliving those cherished memories, surrounded by familiar sights and sounds from my childhood, but this time, I had my dearest friends with me.

I realized that even though time had passed, our bond was still as strong as ever. It reminded me of the closeness we shared.

We tried our luck at various games and won prizes, danced to the music of the live band, and watched as the snow-covered trees sparkled like diamonds in the light. Everywhere I looked, there were smiling faces and cheerful voices, all united in the spirit of the season.

As the night wore on, I felt a bittersweet mixture of joy and sadness. I knew that soon I would have to leave my friends and return to my own life, but for now, I could only be grateful for this moment of connection and shared memories.

The winter festival had brought me back to a place of warmth and belonging, reminding me of the love and laughter that I had missed so much. It was a magical place, with its bright colors and sparkling lights, and I knew that this memory would stay with me for a long time to come.

"Oh, we got to go. I just got notification that our reservation is almost ready," Curtis said, taking another bite from his kebab.

***

Stepping into Gogi Byeokje, the first thing that hit me was the smell - a mouthwatering aroma of sizzling meat and spices that made my stomach rumble. The Korean Barbecue restaurant was filled with the sound of sizzling

grills, clinking glasses, and lively chatter.

The walls were adorned with colorful posters and photos of various celebrities that visited, and the tables were fitted with built-in grills and exhaust fans. Since we had reservations, it was quick for us to get a table and order.

Curtis purposely didn't eat much the entire day for this moment, hoping to get a little tipsy from the alcohol before his stomach fills up.

The menu was a feast for the eyes, with a wide array of options ranging from traditional Korean dishes like bulgogi and galbi to fusion dishes like kimchi quesadillas and Korean fried chicken. Leslie immediately took charge of the ordering. We started with some appetizers, like the crispy fried dumplings and spicy Korean wings. We couldn't resist trying a bit of everything.

As we ordered, another server brought over plates of banchan - small side dishes like kimchi, pickled vegetables, and bean sprouts - to accompany our meal. The grills were fired up, and soon our table was filled with the sizzle and smoke of cooking meat.

We took turns grilling, using tongs to flip and turn the pieces to perfection. The marinated beef and pork were tender and juicy, bursting with flavor, while the chicken and seafood were crisp and savory.

Beverly kept herself busy cooking slices of beef on the grill, while Leslie chatted away about her and Rose's recent trip to Japan.

Meanwhile, Curtis and Jason were playfully bantering with each other over a game on their phones, while Rose poured separate drinks for everyone except Beverly who had her tea.

When the server came by to see if there was anything else we'd like to order, Leslie, who was always the most adventurous when it came to food, suggested we try the ox tongue. I hesitated at the idea, but decided to give it a try. Surprisingly, it was quite delicious.

I grabbed another piece from the grill and savored the explosion of flavor in my mouth. I couldn't help but smile as I observed my friends relishing the food and each other's company. Curtis showed us how to properly dip the meat in the sauces and wrap it in lettuce with kimchi and rice.

I took a sip of my strawberry soju, debating on how to break the ice with friends I haven't seen in so long. I'm not really good with sudden conversations, especially with people I haven't seen in years, let alone at a table where we're all eating.

"So Curtis, how's the office life working for ya?"

Jason glanced at me and winked, sipping away at his soju. *Thanks for the save.*

"Surprisingly, good. I never really thought I'd be into it, but at least it beats working overtime shifts at the last job. I barely had a social life."

Curtis is currently employed as a full-time project manager at a major firm located two hours away in upstate. I recall that before we graduated high school, he had applied to college as an engineering major, but it seems he made a switch to accounting at some point. Back then, whenever we bumped into each other in the hallway between classes, he would passionately discuss stocks and the economy, so this career shift suits him much better now.

We were both the quiet, bookish types and bonded over our love for fantasy novels. I remember we used to spend hours at the library, discussing our favorite authors and characters.

"I'm hoping to finally buy a house. I've managed to save up enough, thanks to my debt finally being cleared. I figured it was about time to reap the fruits of my labor and settle down a bit." He proudly raised his beer, taking a sip. "Since we're on this topic, what's new with you guys?"

Yep, as I expected. Whose gonna go first?

Without a word, Leslie and Rose placed both their hands on the table tightly interlocked together. On Rose's finger shined a vibrant solitaire diamond ring.

"We were gonna tell everyone eventually, but…"

"Congratulations!!!" We all exclaimed.

Beverly was quick to hug Rose and Leslie together. Rose, squeezed between them, tried to sip her drink as her face got all red.

"Since it's two women getting married, do both get an engagement ring or…"

Before Curtis could even finish, Leslie wrapped her arm around his neck roughly rubbing his black hair.

"Hey! Don't crack my glasses! I was just asking a curious question!"

"It's a stupid ass question if you ask me!"

I couldn't help but chuckle. This was exactly how they behaved back in school. Curtis seemed to have a knack for deliberately getting under Leslie's skin, much like siblings teasing each other, and it was always Rose who stepped in to separate them when they started quarreling. That's how Rose and Leslie's love story began.

At the time, they might not have been aware, but I'm certain Leslie was the first to recognize her feelings for Rose, especially given her extroverted nature. She had a habit of speaking her mind with honesty and sincerity.

Rose intervened, pulling Leslie away from Curtis, and their eyes exchanged a knowing glance that acknowledged their affection.

"Anyway, let's drink to that shall we?!" Curtis raised his glass once more, and we all lifted ours in celebration.

"So, who proposed to who?"

"Don't ruin the moment Curtis!"

Curtis tried to keep his composure, but I could see he was holding back the pain he badly wanted to let out after Leslie stomped her heel down onto his foot. He chugged the remainder of his beer before flagging down a server to order another round for the table.

"Just another herbal tea for me," Beverly requested.

"What? No sake for you?"

"A glass of plum sake sounds amazing if I could, but it's not recommended to drink any alcoholic beverages right now."

She tenderly caressed her stomach in soft, gentle circles. It took a moment for all of us to catch on, especially Curtis and Leslie, before Leslie pounced with excitement. Once again, Rose found herself caught in the middle. *I'm sure she regrets sitting there.*

"I'm so happy for you!!!"

Rose gently pushed Leslie away, seeking some breathing space. Her reserved demeanor balanced well with Leslie's quick temper.

Beverly blushed, her cheeks turning pink, as she gazed down at her womb. She was still in the early stages, just three and a half weeks since confirmation, which explains why none of us had even noticed.

"Whose the lucky guy?" Jason asked.

"No one. I did a donor insemination."

The person Beverly wanted to marry and have kids with didn't share the same desire. So, to avoid wasting each other's time on a dream they no longer shared, she ended the relationship. She attempted online dating, but that avenue didn't prove successful either.

"I know it's not the traditional way, but I want to be the best mom I can be, even if there's no father present," she said with determination. We all nodded in support and admiration for her strength and courage.

"Picked out any names yet?"

"I did actually, but I'm keep it a secret."

"I guess another congratulations is in order!" Curtis raised his glass as our drinks arrived. We all took a sip, while Beverly enjoyed her herbal tea.

"No matter what, you have us if you ever need anything," Rose reassured her in a gentle voice.

I'm happy to see that Beverly is content with her life. We first met in Ms. Gould's class and continued to share classes ever since. It's not that we were always friends; rather, it's more accurate to describe us as unofficial rivals. She used to be the studious, high-achieving overachiever, openly showcasing her dreams to the world and asserting herself as the best. I, on the other hand, was quite the opposite.

After my dad's passing, I didn't care about many things, especially school. I would just write to stay awake and maintained average grades to simply pass, finding most of what we did redundant. That's where we used to clash heads.

Then one day, Ms. Gould paired us up for an after-school project, giving us the opportunity to truly get to know each other. Initially, I wasn't sure how to perceive her. But as we spent more time together, I started realizing that we shared more in common than we had both initially thought.

We both had a love for reading and frequently exchanged books. Additionally, we shared an interest in playing sports, often partnering up for games during gym class.

But above all, we cherished our conversations about life. We would spend hours discussing a wide range of topics, from our favorite songs to our aspirations for the future.

Looking back on our friendship, I now realize how fortunate I am to have had Beverly in my life all these years. To witness her now, wearing a contented smile while on the brink of realizing a long-cherished dream, fills me with joy.

"You started this Jason, what about you?" Beverly asked, pointing fingers. "How's that documentary coming along?"

"Documentary?"

I glanced at Jason, who was seated beside me, attempting to play it cool while flipping pieces of bulgogi on the grill. With a thoughtful expression, he took a bite, contemplating how to express his thoughts.

"I've been nominated."

While everyone else cheered excitedly, Jason modestly downplayed his achievement. I could only gaze at him in astonishment. How could he not have told me?

I was aware that he was trying to get this documentary off the ground about his family's life as immigrants moving to the States. However, he didn't mention anything beyond that in our text conversations. He was never one to stray from is dreams, no matter the struggle.

"I wanted to wait till the official announcements were made to tell you guys. A friend of mine who's working for the awards told me early."

"Cheers to that!" Curtis exclaimed, raising a strip of pork with his chopsticks in solidarity before taking a bite.

"Ah, it's nothing. It's all thanks to someone's father for inspiring me to pursue anything like this - to have a voice and a story to tell."

There he goes being humble again.

"Besides, I can't overshadow a best selling novelist sitting with us." He looked right at me, took a sip, and winked. Did he really have to put me on the spot?

All this time, I enjoyed hearing about everyone else's accomplishments, but being in the spotlight feels awkward, and I don't know what to say. I clasped my hands between my thighs for a moment before downing my drink. I hadn't mentioned to any of them about my new novel that recently hit the bookshelves, titled '*Asimo*'.

The story revolves around a humanoid robot named Asimo, who has achieved singularity. It becomes a spectacle to behold and a star attraction for a robotics company. People are awed by its human-like appearance and intellect. However, Asimo yearns to be free and live like any other being. Exhausted by its role as a circus attraction, it makes a daring escape during an expo presentation, driven by desire to pursue the dreams it always had.

"I've read the book twice already," Beverly exclaimed. "That ending was very powerful."

"Don't spoil it! I'm only on chapter three," Rose said.

Leslie chimed in, "You're going to have a book signing party, right?"

I blushed at the attention, but was secretly pleased at their praise. "I don't know about any signing party. But, thanks. I'm sorry I didn't get the chance to tell you guys about it sooner."

At the end of the table, I noticed Curtis discreetly using his phone. I'm sure he's attempting to order a copy and asking Jason where he can get it.

"It's all thanks to your number one fan there for telling us about it," Beverly stated glaring at Jason. He tries to play coy again, sharing a glass with Curtis.

"Curtis you order your copy yet?" Rose asked.

"I'll probably get the audiobook so I can just listen to it while pretending to work."

As we continued eating, we chatted and laughed, enjoying the lively atmosphere and delicious food. The servers came around to check on us, offering refills of soju and beer and making sure we had everything we needed.

***

By the end of our meal, we were stuffed and satisfied, with empty plates and a pile of discarded bones and shells. Leslie patted her belly, sinking back into the booth.

I couldn't eat anymore either as we all were in the midst of catching the itis. It's common and inevitable when eating at an "all you can eat"-style place. I'd be ready for bed right about now.

"It's only 9:30. What do you guys think about going to Midnight Mic after this?"

"I'm stuffed man and now you a want to sing?" Leslie held her stomach, leaning on Rose's shoulder for support.

"For old time sake!"

"I think that would be fun." I subconsciously blurted out without even thinking. *Why did I say that? I barely sing.*

"Javi's down! If Javi's down, of coarse Jason will be…Beverly?"

"If it's to hear you try to sing that one song again and mess up horribly, sure. Besides, I live down the street so it's easier for me going home after."

"See, Leslie?"

Leslie glanced at Rose, who was minding her own business and taking one last bite of her food. She spoke with the tail end of a shrimp still hanging out of her mouth.

"You can sleep on the couch while I sing the song we picked out for our wedding."

"Who said I'm going to be the one sleeping?!"

We split the bill and got up from the table. As we walked, I slowly stayed behind everyone else, capturing this small moment in my head. The experience had been more than just a meal - it was a chance to connect with friends and a feast for the senses. *It truly feels like I never left.*

4

Midnight Mic is a highly popular karaoke bar in town and one of the many hotspots for adults to enjoy on the weekends.

The last time all of us were here was before we left for our separate colleges. I'm not very fond of singing, but with a group of friends in a private room, all singing terribly together, is pretty fun.

We entered into the dimly lit karaoke bar and immediately I was hit with a wave of excitement and anticipation. The air was thick with the sound of music and energy. The hallways adorned with neon light, beckoning us to our room to sing to our hearts content.

The bar itself was bustling with activity, with bartenders expertly mixing drinks and servers weaving their way through the crowd to deliver orders to each room. The menu offered a variety of snacks and appetizers, perfect for nibbling on between singing sessions.

While all the other rooms were occupied with a variety of song genres, their echoes reverberated through the walls as Curtis selected the first song. The bar boasted an extensive collection of songs in different languages, from classic oldies to contemporary pop hits, ensuring there was something for everyone. The top-of-the-line karaoke system projected lyrics onto a large screen that illuminated the room. At the same time, Jason returned from the lobby bar.

"I ordered us a round of sake since we might be here awhile. Beverly, the owner was kind enough to make you fresh pineapple juice."

"Much appreciated."

Curtis entered the song number on the screen, and the instrumental track began to play.

The instrumental had a lively and upbeat tempo, with a prominent bass-line driving the rhythm. There are also electric guitar riffs and a bright keyboard melody layered on top, adding to the overall energy of the song. The drums are crisp and precise, providing a steady foundation for the other instruments to build upon. Overall, it's a fun and catchy instrumental that gets people dancing and singing along.

Curtis takes off his glasses and began to sing.

"I stepped up to the mic, feeling brave. Ready to sing, and to misbehave. Bum. Ba. Da Da," he sings to the rhythm. He is trying. "But as the music started, I lost my way. And suddenly I had nothing to say. Da. Da. Ba. Bum."

Leslie laughed.

"Wow, I didn't know you had such a great singing voice," she said sarcastically.

"You're up next Les…My voice cracked like a teenage boy. And the lyrics just seemed to annoy. Ra. Da. Da. Ha! The crowd looked bored, they wanted to leave. And I knew then, I was gonna grieve. Oooooooweeeeeeeeeeeee!!!!"

It felt like hours passed since we started. As I watched my friends belt out the lyrics to their favorite songs, I couldn't help but smile. The room was filled with the sound of laughter and singing, and the atmosphere was infectious.

Leslie and Rose took the microphones next, having already sung multiple times already. They approached the microphones with confidence, their voices blending seamlessly, and the rest of us cheered them on.

Beverly and Curtis were busy scrolling through the song list, trying to decide what to sing next. Curtis was flipping through the pages with a grin, while Beverly looked over his shoulder with a playful smile.

They took the mic next and sang their hearts out for several songs while we continued to enjoy our drinks. I took a sip and leaned back in my seat, immersing myself in the vibrant energy of the room.

Beside me on the couch, Leslie and Rose were in each others arms, engaged in their own conversation. I found myself staring at the empty glass on the table, gradually tuning out the surrounding sounds. In that moment, I suddenly felt disconnected.

The room began to spin, and the noise around me seemed distant and muffled. The weight of all those drinks finally hit me like a ton of bricks, my head pounding in response. I felt this sudden detachment from the world around me. It was as though I were observing the scene unfold from a distance, instead of being fully present in the moment.

So many thoughts swarmed around in my brain. I began to wander in my head, thinking back to earlier in the day when I read my mother's letter. The memories flooded my mind, and suddenly I couldn't breathe. My heart started to beat faster and faster. I clutched the pendant hidden under my sweater, hoping for some sort of comfort to calm the pulsing in my chest.

It's like I'm trapped in my own body, unable to escape the panic that's overtaken me. I tried to control my breathing, but it only seemed to get worse. Tears streamed down my face as I realized how much I've missed out on by leaving town.

I closed my eyes for a brief second in an attempt to calm myself when I felt a hand touch my shoulder. It's Jason.

"You've been quiet. Thinking about your next book already?" His words brought me back to reality and I realized I had been zoning out for the past few minutes.

"Whaaa? Oh, no. I just…"

"Javi! Your turn to sing, but first, another round of shots!"

For the record, Curtis isn't an alcoholic as this situation may make it seem. He just knows how to party.

"If you go up to sing, I'll do a duet with you." Jason proposed.

"Deal."

I took a deep breath, attempting to shake off the dizziness. I'm here to have fun and enjoy the night with my friends. Downing the shot swiftly, I slammed the glass on the table, feeling reinvigorated and ready to go.

"Hey! Hey! We gotta take it together! I'm pouring you another one!"

Leslie poured me another shot and we raised our glasses together.

"Arriba! Abajo! Al centro! Pa dentro!" We shouted in unison. Glasses clinked as we raised our drinks in a toast to the rest of the fun night ahead.

Whatever bottle Curtis ordered was undeniably strong. Seconds ago, I had managed to handle it without even concentrating on the taste. This time, however, I took note of its potency, and it left a lingering, intense aftertaste on my tastebuds. Each of us had our own reactions, and Beverly, being the only sober one, simply laughed at our faces.

I grabbed the microphone and Jason joined in on the next song, feeling a rush of excitement. My friends cheered me on, and as the night went on, I found myself letting go of my worries and just living in the moment.

The karaoke bar was the perfect place to forget about the stresses of life and just have a good time with the people I missed. The more songs we all sang the more round of shots kept coming until Rose became the first one to fall asleep, her head drooping onto the table as she snored softly.

"And she thought I'd sleep first."

Eventually, the instrumentals just kept playing in the background as we couldn't resist the opportunity for a little mischief, so we took turns drawing silly faces on her with our markers. Beverly drew a monocle and top hat on her forehead, while Leslie added a curly mustache. Curtis opted for a unibrow and a large, goofy smile.

"Wait wait!"

Jason pulled out his phone and we gathered around her on the couch.

Snap! Snap!

We took various group photos in different poses around Rose's sleeping body, giggling like school kids.

Leslie started singing a stirring rendition of "I Will Always Love You" while we bursted out laughing, unable to contain our amusement at the sight of her decorated face.

"This is definitely going into our wedding photo collage." Leslie chuckled.

I guess because I focused so much on leaving, I never thought I'd ever come back for moments like this. This was definitely long overdue to happen.

It reminded me of the fun times I used to have growing up. I felt grateful for my friends who had brought me back to enjoy this moment to the fullest.

The rest of the night was a blur of bad singing, laughter, and more drinks. We took turns performing our favorite songs, cheering each other on and making fun of our own off-key attempts.

Despite the pounding headache and dizziness, I knew I had made new memories that I would cherish for years to come. Part of me wishes I could stay in this moment like a never ending dream.

By the time we left, it was well past midnight. The streetlights illuminated the sidewalk as we exited the karaoke bar.

The winter festival had come to an end with only a few people still walking about. Rose, who had been sleeping on Leslie's shoulder for the past hour, stirred awake and rubbed her eyes.

"Where did all this marker on my face come from?" she exclaimed, looking around at all of us, her face scrunching up in confusion as she felt the marker on her skin.

Rose was looking at herself using her phone camera.

"Babe, you really don't remember? You got really drunk and dared yourself into drawing on your face?"

"What the hell?!"

Leslie had grabbed a few hand wipes from the restaurant earlier and used one to wipe Rose's face. Curtis checked his watch.

"I have to go. I work in a few hours!"

"Go! Go! I've already hailed a cab."

"It was good seeing everyone. Get home safe." Curtis hugged each of us goodbye and headed towards his car.

"Don't get pulled over rushing home!"

"I'll be fine. Oh Javi, I'm read your book. I got a copy delivered to my office."

"Look at you mister fancy," Leslie teased.

"Till next time! We should do this more often."

And just like that, Curtis had left. Minutes later, Leslie's cab arrived, and with Rose, left next. We all exchanged hugs and they both expressed how much fun they had tonight. I could tell they were still a little drunk, but Leslie knows how to handle these situations.

"Goodnight, y'all." Leslie yawned.

"Get home safe you two! And congratulations again!"

Rose added, "We have a lot of wedding planning to do tomorrow. Let's do this again soon, guys!"

The cab drove down the street, disappearing around the corner. Beverly was the last to say goodbye since she only lived right at the corner. She hugged both Jason and I at the same time.

"It's been so long you guys. I'm so glad to see you both doing well. And Javi, promise you'll come visit more often."

"I promise."

"I'll hold you to that. This will always be your home. Take care, you two."

We watched her walk to the corner, entering inside the building. Jason and I stood in front of the karaoke bar as they prepared to close as well with people leaving.

"I don't know if you have time till the last train, but do you want to grab coffee?"

"You know I don't drink coffee."

"Yeah, but how often do I get to spend time my best friend? Besides, you can share your ideas on the next book."

"You'll have to wait like everyone else. I'm not even near a draft yet." I retorted, berating a sigh of relief, then followed behind the persuasive hazelnut hair.

5

Snow started to lightly fall from the sky. We arrived at the only cafe in town that was still open this late at night.

From the outside, it looked folksy and clean. White painted bricks made up the building's outer structure. It's warm light shined outside the glass windows with passionate voices from within echoing outside.

According to Jason, it's the one place all artist and aspiring writers go for that extra late night boost or to wind down. It definitely had the cafe atmosphere.

As we entered, we're welcomed by the amazingly brewed scents. The barista was quite busy but still managed to welcome us with a wave.

I lounged in their bean bags feeling lifted by clouds. It's definitely a nice creative space to let the mind flow with a nice cup of strawberry chai.

Several patrons were sitting with headphones on, hovered over their laptops, typing away. This cafe had several PCs stationed on the second floor where lots of people were going for isolation and focus. *How big is this place for an Internet cafe?*

Jason handed me a dragonfruit refresher before sitting beside me in another bean bag, sipping his iced coffee and browsing through his phone.

"You didn't have to get me anything."

"Trust me, you'll need something to counter all the alcohol from earlier."

We sat back with our drinks and dosed away as the aromas and silence took effect.

It felt good to relax after the long day we'd had. Karaoke was a blast, but all that singing and drinking left me feeling drained.

This was the perfect spot to unwind and I could feel my mind clearing up and less tense, slowly sinking into a sleepy state. My head stopped pounding from earlier after every sip I took.

As I looked around the dimly lit room, I couldn't help but feel a sense of nostalgia. Internet cafes like this one used to be so popular back when we were in high school. I remembered spending hours at one with Jason, Beverly, and Curtis, playing online games and chatting with strangers in voice chat from all over the world. It's funny how times had changed, but some things remained the same. *I could sleep here.*

I took another sip of my drink, sinking further back, closing my eyes for a moment. The warmth of the bean bag chair and the soft chatter of the other patrons was oddly soothing. I felt my muscles relax and my mind completely clear, and for a brief moment, everything felt right in the world.

"Don't fall asleep yet. There's something I wanted to show you."

Jason got up, pulling me along. My whole body felt like dead weight not wanting to stand at all.

"Do I have to?"

"It's something cool. I promise."

"Fine."

I followed behind him as we went into a room below the stairwell where it was much darker than the rest of the cafe.

"Where are we going?"

"Just listen."

The tranquility of the cafe was immediately disturbed by a burst of loud noises. But these weren't just any random cacophonies; they were the vibrant sounds of melody. We ventured into what appeared to be the cafe's basement, greeted by a cascade of neon lights that bathed the room brimming with arcade cabinets.

We both stood at the entrance, my attention completely captured by the classic games I remembered playing as a kid.

"When the town's arcade shut down, this cafe kinda salvaged any of the arcade cabinets they could. The owner is also a huge gamer and grew up playing these so he wanted to keep his childhood alive somehow. This is why the cafe stays open so late. Lots of people still come here to wind down after a long day."

I gazed at the rows of machines with colorful pictures on the sides each with their own tune. My inner gamer was in paradise. "This is amazing."

"…Yeah."

We wandered through the entire room. There were a few people focused playing, but I just kept looking over their shoulders. I felt like a kid again, roaming the aisles, looking at the various arcade games I played with either my parents or friends. They even managed to salvage a few classic pinball machines, even ski ball.

"*Lightning Command*! My dad used to kick my butt in this game."

"Look, they even have *Cooking Instinct*."

"I could never get around the mechanics."

"It's chefs fighting each other while trying to cook a recipe in the kitchen. Felt pretty simple to me."

I kept looking at *Lightning Command*. My Dad and I spent hours in the arcade one summer and this was one of our favorite games to play besides *Mysteries in Darkness: Tales of Mysteria*.

My love for the arcade was because of him. He had nearly every system imaginable, even the VR stuff, and we had so many game nights with Mom. When they found out I made friends, they'd make sleepover plans so my friends could stay the night and play with me.

"Follow me. There's something you gotta see."

Jason grabbed my hand and led me to the back corner where an arcade cabinet stood unoccupied.

The cabinet was predominantly black with yellow accents and featured bold, stylized lettering for the game's title. The theme music felt familiar.

On the screen appeared two fighters in combat in an alleyway. Their 2D-pixel models exchanging blows before the logo appeared on screen: Urban Fighters 8: The Third Impact.

"It's not Mysteries in Darkness, but it's still a classic."

"I could never get over the fact they had so many numbers in the title."

"It's just different versions of the game till the next official installment comes out."

I hovered over the joystick pad for player one, gently touching the buttons, pretending to play. The joystick and buttons were well-worn, a testament to the countless hours people spent playing the game. I looked down where the coin slot awaited a coin's insertion.

"Wait, I forgot all these games take quarters."

Jason plopped down a small bag onto the arcade cabinet. A few quarters started to fall out of the plastic.

"Someone came prepared."

"Well, you are long overdue for beating me the last time."

He inserted two quarters into the coin slot, prompting the screen to flash. I took over player one, while he took two, and I pressed start.

The character select screen appeared and we picked through a diverse selection of fighters. Urban Fighters was a very popular fighting game in the gaming community that centered on street fights in the city under belly.

The use of combos and special attacks unique to each fighter while using the environment to your advantage was a big draw to many who played. It just so happened the version we were playing is the most popular one and beloved by all fans.

The last time I played was against Jason, long before the old arcade was shut down, where we had entered the community tournament that was meant to bring more players in.

The tournament was intense with all kinds of challenging players who surely polished up their skills to show off against others. However, Jason and I were prepared for that, and we bested everyone to where it was just the two of us left in the finals.

This was all before my Dad fell ill and was in the hospital so he watched, dragging Mom along to cheer on too, as Jason and I went toe to toe for number one.

It's easy to tell who won, but after that tournament was when my Dad started to show signs of his illness taking effect. I was so busy trying to keep him here beside me, I didn't bother picking up a joystick again.

"You remember how to play?"

"It'll come back to me."

The screen displayed the vivid and colorful graphics of the game with a satisfying, retro glow. The speakers on either side of the screen emitted the sounds and music of the selected stage, from the crack of fists colliding to the cheers of the crowd in the background.

Round One! Fight!

Our characters began to exchange punches as we inputted the commands. Clearly, Jason has been practicing, fluidly moving his fighter through combos, as I tried blocking to prevent any major health damage. The chip damage was effective, but I had to move onto the offensive and get the upper hand.

As I moved my character, the great undercover detective Naoto Sakura, a lot of her combos started to come back to me.

Her signature weapon is her pistol, that covers not only range, but if you manage to string it well into a combo it can do a hefty amount of damage.

I turned the joystick back, then forward, and pressed the light punch button to activate her special attack that does a good amount of damage to Jason's character. We were close in health now.

"Okay. Okay. I'll take that."

"I'm not as rusty as you think."

"Yeah? I hope you didn't forget this then."

Jason's character teleported behind me in an instant and swung a heavy uppercut into the air, leaving Naoto airborne for a moment before she slowly slammed into the ground. My health was down to zero in just that one heavy attack.

Player Two Wins!

Jason did a short victory dance that he'd usually do when he wins. *Okay the gloves are coming off now.* I loosened up and got closer to the screen - my face focused and ready.

"Uh oh. Someone's dusted off their game face."

Round Two! Fight!

I was aware of Jason's play style especially with this character. Daftmonk Bobby, the wandering nomad monk, had a fighting style that's mostly grappling and heavy attacks, but the developers gave him teleportation which instantly spelled trouble. Not for me though.

The best part about Naoto is she has the ability to set what I call *"trigger traps"*, which are proximity mines that if you get too close, the trap activates and damages the opponent. And the best part is the opponent can't see them until it's too late.

So far, Jason had been keeping his distance due to falling for my traps numerous times when the round began.

Keeping him at a distance left him unable to get close and vulnerable to my range attacks, and even if he tried his teleport, I had a trap waiting for him.

I closed in and initiated the commands for Naoto to unleash her special move where she trapped Daftmonk and unleashed a barrage of roundhouse kicks before firing a shot from her signature pistol.

Player One Wins!

I mimicked Jason's victory dance as he stared baffled by his loss.

"It's not over."

"Oh, I'm warmed up now it's going to be."

I prepared myself for another bout as the both of us were ready to take the win. Naoto takes a few steps back allowing Daftmonk to teleport himself up to stand. Both characters get into stance.

Round Three! Fight!

Both of us were cautious of each other, slowly making calculated moves. He wasn't letting me have any sort of distance or room to place down a trap.

I had to play along with his style and adapt to the situation by using Naoto's kicks to keep him from trying to grapple.

Our eyes did not diverge from the screen at all as our health bars were slowly going down to zero. I'd definitely consider it a close call, for if one of us slipped up with a mistake, that guaranteed the other's victory. However, I had a plan.

I waited for an opening to make a distance between us and anticipated his next move.

"I won't fall for that again."

He, surely, assumed I was making distance to place a trap, but I wasn't. What I knew, that Jason didn't, was the amount of frames it took for Daftmonk to teleport behind me was enough time for me to lay down a trap just before he'd appear.

So I awaited for the opportune moment to come when Daftmonk instantly vanished, turning Naoto to the opposite side and placed down a trap just below where the monk would appear.

BOOM!

Player One Wins!

Once again, I did Jason's victory dance while taking a sip of my drink. He's still shocked of my sudden win.

"How many times have you been here to practice for this moment again?"

"I'll give you that one."

He raised up another quarter.

"Rematch?"

"Best believe it. Don't feel too hurt when you lose again."

I grabbed the quarter, inserted it into the coin slot, signifying I was ready. He followed suit and we were back on the select screen. I, of coarse, selected Naoto again and awaited for Jason to pick Daftmonk, but he didn't.

"What are you doing?"

"Fun fact: I found out this game had a secret character that not many knew about. I had to read a lot of forums to find out how to get him and took a lot of practice attempting to unlock."

"You're pulling my leg."

"No…I…am…not."

Jason inputted a combination sequence, using only the light and heavy attack buttons, causing the arcade cabinet to emit a ringing sound.

On screen, a hidden slot appeared beside the character select where a lone character icon sat. The name appeared on screen: Zephyr.

"Whoa."

He had the appearance of an experienced brawler with integrated technology covering his upper body in a sleek carbon fiber.

In all the years I've known about and played this game, this was a first. He looked so cool.

"This is the only game he's ever appeared in for the series which is why not many people knew about him. When I stumbled upon this forum for the game, a lot people were finding out about him during a few play throughs, so I kinda wanted to see for myself. It wouldn't have been right if you didn't know too."

"Is this why we came here?"

"Yes? Kinda? Plus, I needed payback for that 'L' you gave me back at the tournament."

"For what it's worth, I'm cool with the fact I skipped the last train for this. I can take the first one out in the morning."

"Hope you've warmed up cause I had lots of time testing him out. Be ready."

"Oh just select the stage already. I want to see how he plays."

Round One! Fight!

The stage was set in the heart of a bustling city, with skyscrapers looming in the background and the sound of traffic and sirens filling the air.

The fighting arena composed of a wide, open space surrounded by a chain-link fence, with crowds of cheering spectators on either side.

There were various interactive objects and hazards scattered throughout the arena, such as parked cars, dumpsters, and fire hydrants. Some of these objects can be used as weapons or thrown at opponents, adding an extra layer of strategy to the fights.

Naoto and Zephyr stood a distance apart from one another as the stage music started. Jason and I awaited for the other to strike first.

I knew nothing about this character so I wanted him to make the first move. His character stood calm like a retired professional boxer whose never lost touch of his craft. Jason finally made the first strike.

In a swift second, Zephyr zoned in close for a light attack I wasn't ready for. I had my character create a distance to fire my range attack, but Zephyr instantly blocked it with barely any chip damage taken.

"That won't work on him. Fun fact: the developers implemented that, due to his augments, any range attacks won't do any chip damage to him."

"..."

He's taunting me now. I couldn't have it. I switched to the offensive and zoned in on Zephyr for a quick combo, but Jason anticipated it, leading with a parry, before dealing a hefty amount of damage. I was already below half of my health while Jason still was close to full.

The more the round progressed, I started to learn about Zephyr's moves.

He's more of a close range fighter with his boxing style and can deal long ranged attacks with his special that can keep you on your toes if not careful.

I tried keeping my distance, but Jason kept zoning in. It was like I was playing a completely different player from before. The round ended with Naoto on the ground defeated.

Player Two Wins!

"We're just getting started," I said with determination.

"Try me."

Round Two! Fight!

The stage changed as day turned into night, with the neon lights of the city creating a vibrant backdrop for the action.

Occasionally, a passing car or helicopter will cast a spotlight on the fighters, briefly illuminating their intense expressions and flashy moves. *This game was truly ahead of its time.*

I got a good foundation on how Zephyr played that this round wasn't going to be so easy to win. I immediately went on the offensive to get a lead in damage which took Jason off guard for a moment. That's all I needed to get ahead.

I knew if I stayed too close with a barrage of light and heavy attacks he'd manage to parry. So, I immediately had Naoto jump back, leaving a trap for when he stepped forward.

"Oh no you don't."

He saw through it. Zephyr jumped over the trap and zoned in, leaving my character wide open for a punishing combo. I quickly blocked the attack, but the chip damage dealt was far more than the other characters.

We were neck and neck on health. I wasn't going to let that intimidate me. I fired a barrage of ranged attack combos before having Naoto jump over him.

"You won't push me into a corner."

I kept the distance as I planned my next strategy of attack. I didn't want Jason to see I was desperate as he zoned in, but I knew he'd get too full of himself and fall for the trap I had set earlier. He ran into it, leaving him wide open.

"Gotcha!"

I inputted a combo attack where Naoto is seen on screen throwing two punches and an uppercut before firing a barrage of bullets to hit Zephyr as he's in mid air. I waited for him to fall into the hit box range where I could chain another combo for extra damage.

"Don't get cocky."

Jason made his character recover and parried just in time before I could do anything. We were both neck and neck again with our health close to zero. Just one combo or super attack would be enough to win for either of us.

For him, using Zephyr, he had the upper hand with the high damage he can deal. I had to take a calculated and cautious approach. Even if I win, there's still the final round and it be a tough fight all over again. *I refuse to lose either so let's see what happens.*

Our characters narrowed in on each other. We blocked each others attacks with accuracy and luckily Zephyr takes chip damage from physical attacks so regardless we were on an even playing field.

Neither of us wanted to give each other distance. This exact moment reminded me of when Jason and I fought in the tournament many years ago.

During the tournament, our characters were neck and neck, the crowd hovered around us watching this intense fight unfold as the both of us were too focused to pay attention to our surroundings.

I can be competitive in games sometimes, especially fighting games. They were my favorite things to play growing up besides single player narratives. I guess anyone could say the reason why I'm so good at them is because I wanted to defeat my Dad who always won against me.

The defining moment where I won back then was due to a certain habit Jason had which was he'd let his guard down trying to break mine after a combo. So, I used that against him and won with my super attack.

Now, the playing field is different. Zephyr is a big factor in his play style change and he doesn't leave much room for his guard to be down. We exchanged combos in hopes of breaking the other's block to no avail. Then, I saw the opportunity by jumping over his character and initiated my super attack.

"I gotchu!"

Suddenly, his character managed to parry just in time before punishing my character by unleashing his own super attack. I had to admit his super attack was pretty cool.

Zephyr uppercutted Naoto, following up with a series of punches, then landing a hard haymaker punch midair.

Player Two Wins!

Zephyr stood declared amidst the roar of the crowd, and Naoto was left to slump against the fence, catching her breath and contemplating defeat. Jason proceeded to do his victory dance as I watched, shaking my head.

"Okay, you won. Do you feel avenged?"

"I've had years waiting for this moment. I'm going to enjoy every last bit."

"Yeah well enjoy it while it last till next time I drop by."

He continued to dance as the title screen reappeared on the arcade cabinet.

"Time flies when you're having fun." I checked the time on my phone and sighed, "I can't believe it's this late. Well, early in the morning if you want to be meticulous."

"Tomorrow isn't here until after you wake up from sleep."

"Who says that?"

"Everyone. Can't change my mind of it. As long as you can persuade everyone, and make them agree, tomorrow can be any day you want it to be."

"What fortune cookie you read that from?"

We went back up to the cafe, bought two more refreshers, and left. I looked back at the building for a

FIGHT

moment. *Yeah, I'm definitely coming back here.*

6

We made our way over to the town square, where the
fountain was still lit up with colorful lights.

We sat on the edge of the fountain, taking in the
night, watching as the water danced in the glow of lights. I
couldn't help but fiddle my thumbs, wondering what to say.

It's been a long time since we spent moments like
this just the two of us, despite keeping up through text and
calls here and there, but it was mostly during holidays and
special occasions. It's much easier talking with a group of
friends or doing fun stuff together, but right now, I felt lost.

"What's been bugging you?" he asked, his voice
soft and kind.

He knows when something is on my mind. I
hesitated for a moment, unsure if I could trust him with my
feelings.

"That obvious?"

"Kinda. You look…lost."

I took a deep breath and decided to open up to him.
There's no point in trying to hide it in any longer, I guess.

"I'm just...feeling torn," I said, my voice barely above a whisper. "I've missed so much time with you guys, and I don't know if I'll ever catch up."

It felt like I was rambling on and on about myself like it was the first time, since my late father, I was able to be fully open. And Jason just listened patiently, his kind eyes fixed on mine.

"You've been through so much alone," he said, his voice soft.

"I guess I'm used to it." I couldn't help but let out a small chuckle to ease the air. Life can be one big joke sometimes.

I could feel him getting upset, taking another sip of his refresher. I placed a hand on his shoulder, a gentle expression on my face.

"Tonight was needed."

The snow started to lighten up to where it barely stuck to the ground. It was a beautiful sight to behold.

The buildings around us were covered in a blanket of white, their lights creating a warm and inviting glow against the cold and dark night.

I couldn't help but feel a sense of peace and tranquility as I sat here with Jason, the snow falling around us like a delicate and magical veil. I looked up at the sky where the stars glimmered under the moonlight above us.

"Things change so much, don't they?"

"Depends on your meaning."

"People…places…everything. I remember when we used to come here as kids - it feels the same as I left but at the same time different. And, that's okay…it feels like a lifetime ago anyway. I don't know, I just figured by now I would've forgotten it all and moved on, hoping people might've forgotten me too."

"But, you'll never be forgotten here."

Jason looked at me with understanding in his eyes. My mouth slightly opened in awe as a tear slowly dripped down my cheek.

"There's plenty of people that remember you and ask me all the time how you are. Sure, some faces come and go. Some faces change. But, most stick around and reminisce the old days that we can't get back."

He wiped a tear off his face. "I'd never forget about you. How could I forget the one person who accepted me for who I am in a world I thought would push me away? Because of you, I felt comfortable in my own skin and being the real me even when I didn't fully understand it myself. I'll never forget that."

"…"

I tried to hold it back, but I couldn't help being lost for words. I felt a lump form in my throat as I realized how much those words meant to me. I had always felt like an outsider, but for Jason to say that I had made a difference in his life was a powerful reminder of the impact we can have on each other.

"You may run from your past and want to let everything go, but that's not what memories are for. Good or bad, they become dreams you get to relive over and over."

"Who said I'd want to relive a bad dream over and over?"

"A wise robot once said, 'Just because my past was full of pain doesn't mean the same will be said for my future'."

I couldn't help but pinch him for trying to use a quote from my book against me. We sat in silence for a few moments, just taking in the beauty of the fountain and the warmth of each other's company. I knew that I would always treasure this moment, this connection, this friendship.

***

We walked down the familiar streets towards the train station, the weight of impending goodbyes hung heavy in the air.

I had us part ways halfway since I wanted Jason to get home and rest. I hugged him tightly, feeling grateful for his presence in my life. "Thank you," I whispered, feeling tears prick at the corners of my eyes.

"I know you have a lot going for you in this new life of yours, but please don't be a stranger. At least visit the people who remember you." His smile warm and genuine.

Neither one of us wanted to let go of the other, but it was time for me to leave.

As I walked away, I felt a sense of peace and belonging, knowing that I still had people here who would always be there for me, no matter how much time had passed.

7

As I made my way to the train station, there was one place I knew I needed to visit before leaving. With a sense of both longing and trepidation, I made my way to the Evergreen Memorial Gardens, the town's cemetery and the place where my parents eternally reside.

As I stood before the iron gates, I couldn't help but feel a pull towards the familiar path that led to the hilltop where my parents were buried.

The early morning mist hung in the air, casting an ethereal glow over the tombstones, as if the world itself held its breath in reverence.

With each step, the crunch of gravel under my feet echoed in the stillness, punctuating the silence that enveloped the sacred space. The soft rays of the sun gently peeked through the branches of the tall tree that stood as a sentinel over my parents' final resting place. Its branches swayed, casting fleeting shadows on the ground beneath. Every step I took my anxiety rose. *Am I ready for this?*

As I reached the top of the hill, I caught my breath, overwhelmed by the sight that greeted me. Their tombstones, side by side, marked the spot where my parents found solace in eternal rest. Fresh flowers adorned the graves, a testament to the love and respect that continued to bloom long after their departure.

I took a moment to absorb the beauty of the scene before me, the golden hues of the emerging sunrise painted the sky in a canvas of hope and renewal.

The air held a gentle chill, invigorating my senses and reminding me of the fragility of life. It was a poignant reminder that time moved forward, even as memories anchored me to the past.

I stood before the two graves, feeling a mixture of sadness, confusion, and longing. The autumn leaves rustled softly in the breeze, as if whispering secrets only they could understand.

I knelt down, running my fingers gently over the engraved names, tracing the letters that held a lifetime of memories. Their inscriptions etched in stone, forever capturing what marked their existence, seemed to come alive in my touch. The weight of their absence pressed upon me, filling the air with a bittersweet longing.

"Mom, Dad," I whispered, my voice barely audible.

There were so many things I wanted to say, so many words left unsaid. My heart ached with the weight of unspoken conversations, unanswered questions that lingered in the depths of my soul. Why did they keep things hidden from me? Why was there so much silence between us?

I closed my eyes, trying to conjure their presence, to imagine their voices comforting me with their wisdom and love. But all I could hear was the echo of my own thoughts, bouncing off the tombstones.

Tears welled up in my eyes, and I wiped them away, feeling the weight of missed opportunities.

"I miss you," I cried, my voice barely a whisper heard amidst the rustle of leaves, quivering with emotions held back for far too long. "There's so many things I never got to say, so many apologies left unspoken…and yet the ache within me still lingers."

I pulled out the necklace that rested underneath my sweater, clasping it in my hands.

"If only I could turn back time…"

The weight of regret settled heavily upon my heart, and I found myself speaking aloud, addressing the departed souls of my parents.

My chest suddenly felt heavy so I took a deep breath to clear my thoughts.

"I thought that if I came here, I could finally find closure and understanding. Part of me wishes I could still just move on, but I can't. Mom, I wish I could truly apologize to you for our growing distance over the years but what's done still lingers heavily. Dad, I miss our late-night talks when life got tough. There were so many times I needed to hear your voice when I felt troubled…Time is a cruel thief, stealing away the chances we had, to say the things that needed to be said. I wish I could have told you over and over how much I loved you, how much I still do."

The realization hit me like a wave crashing against the shore, overwhelming and unforgiving. I had let the bitterness consume me, and now, with nothing but the cold embrace of tombstones surrounding me, I realized the futility of my anger.

The regret I felt was not solely for the words left unsaid, but for the time wasted dwelling on the what-ifs and maybes, the years spent drowning in a sea of resentment.

If only I had mustered the courage to bridge the divide while they were still alive. But life, relentless as it is, does not grant us the luxury of hindsight until it is too late.

Now, standing here, face to face with the reality of their absence, I am left to grapple with the shards of a broken connection, longing for the chance to rewrite what's done.

Tears welled up in my eyes, blurring the images before me, but I knew that my words would reach them, even if only in spirit.

As the sun continued its ascent, casting a warm glow upon the landscape, I gazed at the flowers blooming on their graves where a small blue butterfly gently landed on one of the petals before fluttering away.

With a heavy heart, I rose to my feet, knowing that it was time to continue my journey. The sun had fully risen now, illuminating the world around me with its golden embrace. I took one last look at the graves beneath the towering tree, feeling a sense of gratitude for the love and memories we had.

The sun illuminated my path, casting a warm glow on the road ahead, as if to remind me that even in moments of sorrow, light and hope would always find a way.

I took a deep breath, allowing the cool autumn air to fill my lungs and with a bittersweet smile, I turned away from the gravesite and made my way to the train station. The journey ahead was uncertain, but I knew I had to take it.

As I walked towards the platform, I glanced back one last time, bidding a silent farewell to the place that held the physical remnants of my parents. The train whistle blew in the distance, a signal that it was time to embark.

8

I stood on the train platform, watching as people hurried by, lost in their own worlds. The sun casted a warm glow over the horizon. The air felt crisp and fresh, with a hint of dew lingering in the grass. The grassy fields reflected softly off the sunlight.

There was something almost so therapeutic about looking out at my hometown in the early morning - similar to looking at the ocean on a sandy beach or a forest full of wildlife on a hike.

I took a deep breath, trying to capture the feeling of this moment. I promised myself to comeback for I have friends here that I wish to not forget.

I sat down on the bench beside a woman in a blue dress awaiting the train's first scheduled arrival of the day.

The old brick walls of the platform were covered in faded graffiti, a reminder of the many travelers who have passed through here over the years. A small group of pigeons pecked at the ground, unfazed by the bustle of the station.

Last night really was needed. I couldn't stop thinking about the moments with my friends and being able to laugh with them again. I really did miss them, despite the memories of the past leaving an open wound.

Just the thought of leaving again, I felt a sense of emptiness inside me, like a hole that couldn't be filled. *What if I just moved back and stayed?*

I noticed a man standing nearby, looking out towards the tracks. He had a warm smile on his face, and I could tell that he was waiting for someone.

"Daddy!"

Just then, two little girls came running up to him, arms outstretched, their faces lit up with excitement. The man scooped them up into his arms, laughing.

"Hey! Oh my god! Alright Alright haha."

"We missed you."

The girls chattered excitedly, telling him all about the winter festival they had just been to. They talked about the lights and the music, the hot cocoa and the ice skating.

"Let's go to the bakery on the way home!"

"Can we? You gotta try this year's gingerbread cake, Dad. It was so good."

The man's wife walked up to them, smiling as she watched the reunion. They hugged and kissed, and the family made their way towards the exit, the girls still chattering away about the festival.

As I watched them go, I felt a pang in my heart, serving as a poignant reminder.

Throughout my life until now, I've often felt isolated and adrift, as if I didn't quite belong in this world anymore.

I couldn't help but constantly wonder what my life would have been like if things had been different, if my parents were still alive and if we were still a complete family. These thoughts perpetually occupied my mind. What if my earnest wish had come true?

It almost feels as if the universe is sending me a constant reminder, a sign, to reflect on these thoughts and emotions.

It was hard not to get lost in memories of happier times, but much harder to forget the pain that followed in their absence.

My thoughts returned to the letter my mother left me, and the mention of a long gone sister named Leah. It's been stuck on my mind this entire time. Could things have been different if she were alive today? Would she have been able to bring me back home? Would we have been able to heal the wounds that caused our family to be torn apart?

Maybe I should've never left. I only did so because I hated everything. I felt like no one cared and that time stopped for me. I could never get that back.

At first, I just wanted to leave my memories behind, but now I wish I could redo it all over again just differently.

Only if things were different.

All these years I still haven't been able to shake the fact that even the slightest action or word spoken brought this bearing on my heart. If I could start over again, I would. If I could change, I would. Even then, it's still hard to let go…

Chooooooooo!

As the train pulled up to the platform, I took a deep breath and boarded via the rear doors, feeling the weight of my loneliness pressing down on me. I knew that I had to keep moving forward, even if it felt like I was walking alone in the dark.

9

The doors hissed shut and the train set off again.

On board, I sat backwards into the nearest open seat by the window feeling a mix of emotions as we departed the station.

In a matter of seconds, my hometown grew smaller and smaller in the distance as I embarked on my journey back into the vast open world once more.

A sense of sadness and nostalgia came over me, acknowledging that once again, I was leaving behind the people and places that had shaped me into who I am today.

As the sun rose higher into the sky, casting a warm golden glow over the landscape outside, I scrolled through the pictures we had taken last night. There's a photo of us at Gogi, all grinning like fools as we stuff our faces with bulgogi and kimchi.

In another photo, we're crowded around singing karaoke, with Leslie and Rose belting out a duet while the rest of us cheer them on. I could never delete the photos of us surrounding Rose asleep on the couch it's easily a classic.

And then there are the photos from the winter festival, where we're all bundled up, posing in front of the brightly lit parade floats. There's even a photo of me and Jason, snowflakes falling gently around us as we grin at each other like a couple of dorks in front of the brightly lit Christmas tree.

We had our moments where we laughed, sung and danced together, creating memories that I will cherish forever. Just then, my phone buzzed constantly courtesy of Leslie creating a group chat with all of us in it.

Thanks for coming by Javi!

Hope you have safe travels on the train!

Get home safe! It was good seeing you again.

Text us when you get home!

When did you guys take these pictures?!

Make sure you keep your promise and come back!

There was a promise? Well in that case next time we're going to Zen Den Hour.

Curtis, shouldn't you be at work!

I smiled, feeling this sense of connection to my friends even though we were now miles apart. I still can't believe that despite missing so much time with them, we still act like nothing changed at all.

My phone buzzed again. It was Jason, sending the picture we took together at the fountain. He messaged:

Remember we'll always be here for you. Better keep your promise, I intend to beat you again.

Right then, the train all of a sudden shook violently, jolting me out of my reverie. I looked around, feeling a sense of panic rising in my chest as the other passengers murmured worriedly to each other. *Maybe it was just a bump.*

The train shook again and a few passengers that were standing slammed straight into the floor. I held onto my seat tightly, peering out the window. The train had picked up speed, accelerating at a rapid rate. Something was wrong.

"The trains not stopping." A concerned passenger worried.

We sped pass the next stop and the train continued going. I moved to the next train car, quickly messaging my friends, telling them about the situation. They responded with concern and confusion.

Tell us you're okay!

What's happening?

Plz keep us updated.

Jason meet me at the police station.

The train jolted once more, causing my phone to slip from my grasp and tumble beneath the seats, just as I was about to send my message.

I knelt down, searching, while the constant sound of text pings filled the air as my friends sent messages. *This all must be a minor malfunction and the train will eventually slow down. I could tell everyone I'm okay.*

My heart started beating rapidly. I'm afraid. *This is not how it ends for me. I can't let this be the end.* I thought.

I tried to keep my cool, to stay calm and rational, but it was getting harder and harder as the train continued to shake and rattle.

The phone rang as I found it under the seats. It was Jason. I held the necklace close to my chest, about to answer the phone, when the train lost control and derailed.

In that moment, everything seemed to slow down. The world tilted sideways and my body flew midair alongside the other passengers on board.

Suitcases, bags, and other passenger's personal belongings floated around us as the train tumbled off the tracks. The twisted metal and shattering glass filled my ears, and I knew there was no escape.

This isn't how it ends. I...I...

My last thought was of my friends and family, of the life I had left behind. I saw myself as a child, running through the forest with my dog, laughing with my friends, cherishing the small moments I had with my parents. I saw the people I loved and cared for, and I felt this overwhelming sense of sadness that I'll never see them again.

I wanted to deny my death, clinging to the hope that somehow, someway, I would make it through this. But deep down, I knew that it was unlikely. And so I closed my eyes,

waiting for whatever came next.

I experienced a sharp surge of pain, followed by a thunderous clap, and then nothing. In an instant, everything went black and my life came to an end.

10

My consciousness was slowly fading away. A void of darkness was all that was left, with nothing but the echoes of everyone's screams and cries surrounding me. Then, it stopped.

"So, this is what death feels like," I thought. I felt cold.

Is this really what death feels like? Just a cold empty abyss of nothingness? Not a sound could be heard anymore - not even my own voice. My senses seemed to fade away, and I couldn't see or hear anything. If I felt alone before, I truly am now.

Where am I?

The longer I stayed in this void, the more disorienting it became. I tried to move, but my body felt heavy and unresponsive, as if I was anchored to the spot. My face, my legs, my chest, everything felt numb. I couldn't open my eyes, but there's nothing to even see.

Time started to feel like an eternity as I weightlessly drifted without a sense of direction. I had nothing but time now, I guess. The thought of my life coming to an end and all the decisions I had made up to this point had weighed down in my soul. I wished I could redo it all over again.

I wondered if I had done the right things, if I had made the right choices. I had nothing but time now to think of the things that could've been - what I should've done. The darkness and the silence made me feel small and insignificant, and I began to question myself.

I didn't know how to escape, and the thought of being trapped in this empty space forever filled me with despair.

All I could do was hope that eventually, something would change, and I would be able to break free from this never-ending darkness.

A faint glow appeared in front of me, illuminating through the void. *I feel light.* Just when I thought there was no hope left, I heard humming in the distance.

"Hello?!" I shouted in hopes of being heard.

I was able to open my eyes, but everything was still a blur. Then, I saw a figure in a white dress with angel wings, humming a beautiful melody. A blue butterfly fluttered past overhead.

I closed my eyes and felt a sudden sense of comfort and warmth wash over me. For the first time in what felt like an eternity, I felt at peace.

Then, everything was dark once again.

HER STORY BEGINS IN

My Heart Your Soul

Afterword

Hello. Firstly, I want to express my gratitude for choosing to pick up this book. It means a great deal to me.

Secondly, it's a pleasure to meet you. I'm De'Shaun J. Ruiz.

The story of *My Heart Your Soul* initially began as a short film project during my college days. However, due to life circumstances, the film never came to fruition. Over time, the concept evolved into something much larger.

As I expanded the story beyond a short film to create a comprehensive game, I had additional ideas that I believed would enhance the narrative. I recognized that these ideas wouldn't be fully explored in the game itself, giving rise to *An Angel Inbetween*, *The Beautiful Things*, and *Memory of Dreams*.

Though I've always aspired to craft a light novel, the length of *Memory of Dreams* didn't align with a full novel format. Thus, I contemplated referring to it as a light novella, serving as the missing piece that connects to the game's universe.

While my intention was to release everything alongside the game's launch, the challenges of financing and development—undertaken solo—led to inevitable stress. I was determined not to present this story as a mere tie-in; I wanted it to hold significance. Consequently, I invested the necessary time to refine the narrative and illustrations to my satisfaction.

I hope that through reading this book, the experience of the game takes on a new dimension, allowing for a deeper connection with Javi.

To my dearest friends who supported me throughout the entirety of *My Heart Your Soul*'s development, spanning from the game, the children's books, the lofi playlists series, and this novella, your belief in me is sincerely appreciated.

To all those mentioned in the game's credits, without you, none of this would even exist. It would remain an idea I'd struggle to bring to life.

To Javi, you carry parts of myself within your character, serving the narrative's purpose. Through your journey, I've come to terms with many things. Like Leah, you will always have a place in my heart.

Lastly, to my readers—those who played the game prior to reading this, and those who will play in the future—the notion of a light novella or the concept of *My Heart Your Soul* might not be universally appealing. Yet, having a select few give it a chance means the world to me. So, I extend my heartfelt thanks. Your support is especially meaningful to me as an aspiring self-publisher and artist striving for professionalism. I did everything myself after all.

This book signifies the finale of the *My Heart Your Soul* story. I sincerely hope that you, as the reader, have gained something meaningful from this experience.

As I embark on my next adventure, I look forward to welcoming you when it unfolds.

Until then.

De'Shaun J. Ruiz

My Heart Your Soul
TOGETHER AGAIN:
THE LOFI SERIES

ADDITIONAL TITLES FROM BIJOU-BOT ENTERTAINMENT

https://www.bijou-botentertainment.com/

MY HEART YOUR SOUL: AN ANGEL INBETWEEN

A girl opened her eyes to find a magical world all around her. Unaware of who she was or why she was there, she explores and discovers this wonderful place. Follow along as she journeys a new world in the Inbetween.

MY HEART YOUR SOUL: AN ANGEL INBETWEEN © De'Shaun J. Ruiz
ILLUSTRATION: Alexandra Silakova
Bijou-Bot Entertainment

MY HEART YOUR SOUL: THE BEAUTIFUL THINGS

Follow this story about loss and the importance of always remembering that no one is ever truly gone.

MY HEART YOUR SOUL: THE BEAUTIFUL THINGS © De'Shaun J. Ruiz
ILLUSTRATION: SANI
Bijou-Bot Entertainment

(AMAZON EXCLUSIVE)

IMPROVASTORIES: SEASON ONE

An anthology series based on the podcast that tells stories through improvisation. Improvastories adapts the podcast into pages for all to read and enjoy.

IMPROVASTORIES © De'Shaun J. Ruiz
Contributions by: Antonino La Rosa, Peter Echevarria, Bryan Aguilar, Kiara Espinal
Bijou-Bot Entertainment

www.ingramcontent.com/pod-product-compliance
Lightning Source LLC
Chambersburg PA
CBHW041736300726
48978CB00001B/10